TAKE ME BACK

Shani Greene-Dowdell

VISIT ONLINE:

www.shanigreenedowdell.com

Chapter One
Blaze

There's a light mist in the air as I make my way across the street towards the alley. I had gotten a call from our tip line stating that a prostitute would be waiting, looking for customers. We're working this area heavy looking for girls we can bust, bring into the station, and then find out who has them out here. The sex trafficking problem is so massive in our city that every time I see a young woman walking the streets after dark, I want to rescue her. Taking this assignment merely is my duty to help fix this massive problem.

Before long, I see a girl standing with her back pressed against the old stone wall in front of a timeworn apartment building. She has one foot propped up on an old stump for support. Her stance shows off the six-inch red heels she's wearing. Besides her being in the location mentioned on the call, I know it's her just by the nasty way she's standing there watching me approach her. Suddenly, wearing a suit that costs

3

more than my truck, and a watch that's even more expensive, doesn't seem like the right move. She'll probably recognize me as a police officer just by looking at me. I start to second guess all of my fancy clothes that are on loan from my homeboy, Terry, who is an investment banker downtown. His clothes are the exact things a police officer would wear when they're trying to fit in. What was I thinking?

"You can borrow this outfit under one condition," Terry had warned me.

"What's that?" I had asked warily. I already didn't want to do this assignment, and he knew it, which is why his response was to further taunt me about it.

"Don't you fuckin' dare get any cum on it. I swear to God, Blaze, I will kill you if I see some on my jacket." He had the nerve to look dead serious.

"What the fuck? I'm not actually going to have sex with these women; you know that, right? I just need to look the part so that I can make a deal with the prostitutes. Then, we're picking them up. So, chill man. It's nothing like what you're thinking."

"Alright, I'm just saying. I don't want cum on my shit, Magic Mike."

4

"Whatever man," I said and gave Terry a *handshake before I made a break for it with the clothes. I didn't want to hear anymore Magic Mike jokes. I should never have agreed to watch that movie with him. I definitely wouldn't have if I knew this assignment was coming up. Magic Mike's not even about prostitutes, either. It's a good thing we didn't watch Pretty Woman—*

My only comfort is the fact the girl I'm about to approach looks even fancier than I do. She has ridiculously big hair with a head of ringed curls, and a thick black sweater dress that hugs onto every curve on her body. Her red heels have to be at least six inches. She's trying too hard like she's using her hair and clothes to cover up the fact that she's just a nervous little girl.

Instead of enraging me, as I would expect it to, seeing her makes me feel protective. I want to wrap the girl up in my coat to cover her up so no one else can see her, take advantage of her, or belittle her. Then, I want to take her home and feed her something warm. *I'm getting soft.*

Despite the overcompensation with her clothing and hair, the vivaciousness in the girl's body is unmistakable. My eyes catch onto her thick-looking thighs and flat stomach, peeking out from the cut of the dress, and my mouth goes dry. It literally feels as if I've been eating cotton. None of what I'm feeling is appropriate for an undercover cop. I'm perving on someone who looks barely old enough to buy liquor.

I should be preparing to turn the girl around and cuff her to send her off to jail, but what I'm thinking about are all the other reasons I could roll her over. Number one, she has a really nice ass.

The closer I get, the more my nerves spike. What the hell was I thinking signing up for this assignment to pick up prostitutes? I guess I wasn't expecting any of them to catch my attention like this girl.

The only thing that helps me relax is the way her eyes keep darting over to a screen in a nearby bar as if she is checking the score of the game to pass the time. It's such a reasonable thing to do that it makes me feel comfortable as I approach her.

"Hey there," I say, once I'm close enough to be heard. My voice comes out thick and husky, surprising me. I sound like I'm trying to be sexy.

Magic Mike… Terry's jokes come back to haunt me, almost causing me to chuckle.

She jumps at the sound of my voice, then seems to catch herself. Licking her lips, she looks up at me through her long lashes. And wow, now that I'm closer, I can see she is far from being a kid. Oh no, this isn't some teenager playing dress-up. She is *all* woman. She looks to be about my age, and she's built like a brick house, which doesn't help my simmering attraction to her one bit. My guilt of lusting over a young girl dissipates quickly and opens the door for me to admire her even more.

"Hey yourself," she says, the sound of her sultry voice causing a stirring of warmth in my gut that I immediately cool down.

I concentrate on my training. *Warm the perp up. Get her comfortable.*

"You lookin' for a good time tonight?" I ask, and instantly I want to cringe. I sound like a sexual predator. *Way to go, Blaze.*

The corner of the prostitute's mouth turns up into a half smile like she's trying not to laugh at me.

"Depends on what's a good time for you," she replies. "And... what's in it for me?"

I can't arrest her until there's concrete proof she'll have sex for money. Therefore, I need a clear statement of intent—a 'you'll have to pay me *this* much for *that*.'

"A better view of that game for one," I say, because my next line is supposed to be something about my cock, and I might die of embarrassment if I have to come out and say it. "I've got a big screen in my bedroom," I add, hoping that bit of innuendo is enough to get the conversation headed in the right direction.

She snorts, giving me a grin that seems genuine, considering how deep her dimples go and how bright her eyes get. She gives me a once-over, and the trail of her doe-looking, hazel eyes burns through my fucking clothes. It's at this very moment I know I'm not made for this. When I talk about sex with a woman, it's about to happen. This cat and mouse game with the intent to catch the mouse in a trap doesn't feel right.

"Tempting. What else ya' got?" she asks, seeming intent on forcing me to ask her for a transaction straight out.

"My bedroom is much cozier than watching the game from out here," I say. Meanwhile, I'm struck by the realization that I *want* to have sex with this woman. If we were in the bar together, and she was anyone else in the entire city, I would be putting it all on the line, trying to take her home by drawing on my real lines, or just manning up and asking her to dinner.

Despite the super provocative clothes she's wearing, I'm attracted to her in other ways. Those doe eyes and that full smile are really doing it for me. But fuck, I'm going to have to arrest her, instead of doing all of the things I'm imagining. What a waste?

"What do you need?" I drawl out, while I fight off a stab of discomfort about setting up the trap like this, so neatly.

My gaze lingers on her plump, golden-glossed lips for a few seconds, still wet from the earlier swipe of her tongue. Staring so intently, I can watch every move as she opens her mouth to form the reply that will allow me to lock her up behind bars. Somehow, without noticing it, I've moved closer to her, so close we're breathing the

9

same air. My breath comes short, and the waistband of my pants feels tight.

"Hey!" someone shouts from an open window behind us, sounding furious. "This is private property! You can't be standing around here doing God knows what! Don't make me call the cops! And, young lady, I'm tired of telling you to leave from in front of my apartment. Have a different man out here every night! Go away, now!"

My mood deflates instantly. Someone like this nosey neighbor called me out here in the first place, and the interruption is a swift reminder that I'm here to do a job—to clean up the neighborhood of prostitution and potential human trafficking activity.

"Fuck!" I say, stepping back from the woman who I'm drawn to like a magnet. It's too early to have my cover blown.

"Shit!" the prostitute says. "She's not going to leave that window until we leave."

We stare at each other for one frozen second before there's another, "Take your business elsewhere!" hurled at us from the old woman.

"That woman is always hollering at me. She's batshit crazy, and I don't feel like dealing with her tonight. I'm out of here," the prostitute says quickly.

I fight the disappointment over the tone of her voice changing from sultry and relaxed to anxious and raspy. I'm about to lose the chance to talk to her any longer. With the way she's running away, I may never see her again.

I glance back at the old lady whose long gray hair blows in the wind as she hangs her head out of her apartment window. Her eyes are about to pop out of her head as she watches to make sure we're leaving. Then, my eyes dart to the prostitute who is walking away quickly. The only relief in seeing her go is the thought that I could wait and arrest someone else who's less tempting.

"Hey! Where are you going?" I can't help but ask, hoping for a fleeting chance she'll invite me to come with her.

"It's too hot out here tonight," she says, meaning the old lady is calling the cops. "Let's meet back up tomorrow night when the chance of us getting arrested is much lower."

"Tomorrow?" *But I want you tonight.*

"Yeah, tomorrow!" she yells back to me. "Same time, but this time at the park around the corner, if you're still interested." She takes off in the opposite direction than I need to go back to my car.

Sadly, even after she hits a corner and disappears, I'm still extremely interested in being with her tonight.

Chapter Two
Ari

Saved by the old hag screaming from her apartment window. Thank God, she always has her panties in a bunch when I come out here to work. That lady's obsession with seeing a black face on her block just saved me from forgetting my purpose of being out on these streets in the first place. It sure isn't to find a lover boy to take home. Yet, a few moments ago, I was ready to risk it all for a handsome face, gorgeous smile, and honey-whiskey voice.

I sigh as I make it to the park and sit down on the bench. I pull off my pumps and wiggle my toes, trying to get some blood to flow back through them. This dress is about to hug the breath out of me, and these shoes are the devil's son. Dressing up like some cheap hooker is not only demeaning, but it's just plain stressful on my body and feet.

I look around to make sure I evaded the last potential John. Something about this guy screams 'I'm a good guy who's just hard up for a roll in the hay.' I hate to take guys like him down. It's the pervy ones who have a wife and kids at home that I live to dismantle. The ones who abuse women, I like to take them down even harder.

I never met a criminal that didn't look like filth in my eyes, but the soft look in this guy's eyes tells me he wants to protect girls out on this corner. Or, is it just me he wants to protect? My instincts are usually good, but everyone gets rusty at some point, so maybe this train of thought means I'm losing my edge. Why else is he out here to buy prostitutes when there should be an avalanche of panties coming his way? There has to be some reason for it, I surmise.

The park is empty when I arrive, so no one has followed me. I sit back on the bench and rub my temples. Then, the beautiful smile of my best friend, Tracyee, invades my thoughts. In times of doubt, thoughts of her always set me on the right track. She is the reason I do what I do.

Tracyee ran away from home at sixteen and went to New York. No one in her family ever saw her alive after she left town. We told each other everything, but I didn't even know she was leaving. Her parents were broken, her brother contemplated suicide, and I was lost without my friend. Then, one night, Tracyee's father called my father to give him an update.

When I saw my father's light-brown face blanche, drained of any sign of life and spirit, I knew he was receiving some horrific news on the other end of that call. At that moment, my gut told me he was about to tell me something had happened to Tracyee. The news still haunts me to this day.

"Baby girl, sit down, I have to tell you something," he said once he hung up the phone. His voice was low and devoid of the energy he'd had before taking the call.

I braced myself for the worst. The look on his face alone was terrifying enough to make me feel the Earth was falling out of orbit.

"What is it, Dad? Why are you looking at me like that? Who were you just talking to?" I asked him a barrage of questions, only because his lips weren't moving fast enough.

He grabbed my hands and held them in his and stared at me.

"Dad, talk to me? What's going on?" I urged.

"It's your friend, Tracyee."

My heart sank, my worst fear being realized.

"What about her?" I asked slowly.

"They found her body," he said, his voice cracking.

"Body? What do you mean…body?" I asked though I knew full well what he was saying to me. My mind just wasn't ready to process that my friend, whom I'd prayed to God above for her safe return, would never make it back to North Carolina alive.

"She's gone, baby girl. Dead…" my father's voice trailed off. "She was killed in New York sometime earlier this year, and her body was found today."

"No! No! Daddy, no! Please don't say that. Don't say that she's dead. It's just not right… please…no!" I lost it after hearing the very thing I had been praying I would never hear. My friend was never coming back. I just kept repeating, "No!" over and over again.

In my heart, I knew my friend was gone the moment her parents came over to talk to my parents and me, asking about her whereabouts. I just felt an emptiness I couldn't explain. Tracyee didn't tell me she was leaving. Maybe because she thought I would rat her out. Still, I figured she would have at least called me once she got settled, even if it was a few weeks later. But it had been months, and the months were turning into a year when we got the news of her murder.

"Her father just gave me the news. She got lured to New York with the hopes of becoming a model. She wanted to make it big and then let everybody know what she'd done. But when she got off the plane, she was met by some guys who were sex traffickers." My father, once again, stared at me with an intense look in his eyes, his mouth hanging open with words left unsaid. Then, I recognized what I saw in his eyes. Fear. He feared he would lose me the same way. He went on to tell me that Tracyee was strong and she fought for her life, but it was a battle she didn't win.

From that moment forward, I decided to fight too. That was the night I chose what I would major in when I went to college. I always wanted to go into criminal justice, but whether I would be a lawyer or an officer was up in question. Tracyee's death let me know I wanted to be on the line, stopping sex traffickers in their tracks.

No matter how innocent these guys look, like Mr. Sexy from earlier, my purpose in life is to hold them accountable for what happens to young, unsuspecting girls who are just looking to follow their dreams, or worse, looking for love. My

17

primary purpose in life is to stop men like him. That's why I will meet him tomorrow. No matter how green he looks, he's out here taking advantage of somebody's daughter, somebody's friend, and I will bring him to justice.

I walk around the corner and get inside my red sports car. It's a gift from my father when I graduated from college. My father didn't want me to come to New York, so I think the car was meant to be a bribe. But he has gotten used to me being so far away from home, and he's here practically every month to check on me.

Speaking of the overbearing men in my life, my cell rings just as I crank up to leave. It's my partner.

"Hello Sloane," I answer dryly. Somehow, I already know he's calling to grill me about not calling him earlier today.

"Hello to you. Don't sound so happy to hear from me, or I might begin to think you consider me as a friend," he says sarcastically.

"What do you want, Sloane? I'm taking the night off."

"You see, that's what I thought until I rode over here and saw your car in the parking lot at the park. So, feed me another line about why you're out here working without your partner again," Sloane hisses.

"I came to talk to the girls from last night, to see what I could find out about their pimp, but they weren't here. Since I didn't plan to deal with any Johns, I didn't think I needed any backup," I reason.

"But you did deal with a guy tonight," he says.

"What are you talking about?"

"The guy that was in your face before the old lady said something to break you two up. I thought I was going to have to rescue you from him. What was up with that?" he asks protectively.

"Damn, what? Have you been following me all night? Are you watching me right now?" I ask, looking around the parking lot and over my shoulder in my car.

"You make me sound like a low-life stalker, but you know that's not the case. I'm not watching you. I'm looking out for you, Yan. There's a difference. I know you're headstrong and will try to work without me, but it's too dangerous out here for that," he argues. "When are you going to get that through your head? Hopefully, before it's too late!"

"I know what's going on out here better than you do, Sloane. Remember, I'm the one that goes into these rooms with men, and you're the one who stands outside waiting for a signal. I'm always closer to death than you are, and I never flinch; I have no fear," I tell him.

"Whoa! That cuts deep. I didn't know you thought of me like that. I think you know better than I do that I would go in with them if I had the right utensils," he says, sounding wounded. "I care about what happens to you. That's why I guard you even when you don't want me to."

"I don't mean to come off rude, and yes, I appreciate you looking out for me. It just can be a bit much sometimes," I acknowledge.

"Well, I want you to know I'm here for you, even though you're always pushing me away. When I vowed to look after my partner, I meant it," he says.

"Thanks, partner. I have your back, too."

"You're welcome, and that's good to hear. Good night, Yan."

"Good night," I say and hang up.

A few minutes later, I drive off, heading home. I see Sloane's car take off in the opposite direction, but as I suspected, when I arrive home, he's already waiting at the edge of my driveway.

"Just making sure you get in safely," he yells out of the window.

I smile, go inside, disarm the alarm, and do a quick search throughout the house. It's all clear, so I come back to the door to let Sloane know it's safe for him to leave. It's a routine we follow most nights, so I'm used to it. Sloane's biggest fear is one of the perps finding out where I live and then coming here to attack me. He would have to be swamped with work for him not to see me home safely. It's become a part of our daily ritual.

"Everything is good, big brother," I say because he treats me as if I'm a little sister he has to guard against the world.

"Sweet dreams," he says, waving before he pulls off with the turbo pipes on his Camaro raging as he rides away.

My house is quiet as I go through the motions of getting ready for bed. Once I lay down, the stranger from earlier tonight comes back to my mind. Somehow, when he was around, he made me forget about the crazy old lady's outbursts. He made me forget my overbearing partner would likely be somewhere close by watching. Heck, he almost made me forget I'm an agent.

Chapter Three
Blaze

I'm five minutes early the next night. When I pull up and get out, I notice the air is even more humid than last night, and the sky is gloomy. I spent the entire drive over lecturing myself about how inappropriate it is to be attracted to a prostitute I'm supposed to be *arresting*. I also reminded myself of how important it would be that I keep it together this time. For some reason, I have a terrible feeling my pep talk won't stick—maybe because I spent much of the morning daydreaming about her golden glazed lips, with just enough plumpness to make a strong man weak, being sucked into my mouth.

Then, I lay eyes on her again. She's sitting on a park bench looking like a modern-day princess. I thought I had it together before I got here, but now my little head is bouncing at just the sight of her. I pace the sidewalk by the rose garden, muttering encouraging, self-control mantras to myself. Mantras that will help me get my head in the game before I even think of approaching her.

You're here to make an arrest, I chant in my mind over and over again. *You're a damn good officer, sworn to protect and serve this community,* I tell myself, though I'm not sure I'll ever gather the constitution to put her in cuffs. *Unless it's for other reasons.*

I quiet my thoughts and approach her.

She's wearing another provocative outfit tonight. This time, a candy apple red dress with glittery sparkles that seem to be melding into her cocoa brown skin. The dress shows off her breasts, and the six-inch red heels on her feet bring her just about to my height when she stands, cellphone in hand. The entire outfit is screaming 'come fuck me,' and the thought of another man touching her chips at a piece of my sanity.

"Hello?" I say to take her attention from the phone in her palm.

"Oh shit," she spits out and freezes like a deer caught in headlights when she looks up into my eyes. "You came," she says sounding extra raspy.

"Yes, why wouldn't I?" I ask.

"I don't know. I know you said you were coming, and I was hoping you would. I'm glad to see you," she rambles.

I have to remind myself it's all an act for her. She gets paid and has probably been trained by a pimp or, worse, traffickers, to seduce men into a stupor. This innocent girl act is likely part of the scheme.

"I'm glad to see you, too," I admit, sounding as if I suddenly have cotton in my mouth. The dryness from me holding it open in awe of her beauty is evident. "I mean, *look* at you. What man in his right mind wouldn't come back to meet you?"

The comment is partially me just doing my job, but mostly I can't help myself. The flirtations with her are genuine. I want her to hear every word, soak it in, and understand her beauty.

She blinks, and the sweep of her eyelashes is spellbinding in the dim light of the lamp overhead.

"I guess you're right," she says, smiling. "Now, where were we last night, again? Remind me."

I step closer and let my voice drop an octave. "We were talking about what I have to do to get you in my bed," I say, cutting to the chase. That's easy enough to do because a larger part of me than I would like to admit wants this bed tango to happen pronto.

"Right," she says slowly. She runs her tongue across her plump lips with the promise of something I wish to have. "I was telling you that, I could do that for just for a hun—"

A loud boom of a thunderclap overhead stops her mid-sentence. It's an ominous warning that comes out so loud she jumps closer to me. Seconds later, it's pouring heavy raindrops that soak us both through our clothing to the skin.

"Shit," we swear in unison.

Where did this rain come from? I don't recall hearing anything about bad weather tonight, but the water is coming down fiercely, and it's freezing. I can see goosebumps dotting across her arms, and one pert nipple, peeking out from the tight fabric of the dress and pebbling under the water.

"*Fuck,*" I say with feeling as my mind races to come up with a backup plan. All I can think

26

about is how much I want to kiss the woman standing in front of me while raindrops coat our bodies.

She looks pornographic with her dress matted to her compact frame. I never really thought I had a type before today, but now I'm perfectly aware that my type is *wet*. I'm going to be jerking off to this mental image for months.

"Tomorrow night," her beautiful voice says with yet another promise to make this, whatever it is, happen the next night.

A tinge of disappointment travels through me, yet, I say nothing. I'm staring at her, struck speechless. I'm frozen in my spot watching her ass dance as she runs away in that tight red dress.

"Let's do it at the Day Eight Motel tomorrow so that we won't get rained out," she yells over the thunder. "Same time!"

By this time, she's almost around the corner. I want to run after her, but I'm overtaken by the thought of us being in a room together. With a *bed*.

Meeting her at Day Eight Motel is going to be a nightmare of a test for my self-control. Only the shock of cold water raining down on me clears

27

my head and stops my thoughts from derailing to all I can do to this beautiful woman with a mattress to spread her out on and a little privacy.

"Are you sure I can't give you a ride?" I ask, a last-ditch attempt to make this happen tonight.

"No, my car is parked right over there." She points to an impressive little red sports car. Whoever has her out here has her out here in style.

"Wait!" I yell.

"Yeah!" She turns to face me, firm breasts being caressed by planes of water.

"What name will it be under?" I ask, stalling.

"Ar-Ari," she says and smiles.

"I'm Blaze!" I yell as she slides into her car.

She rides off before I jog backward in the direction of where I'd parked my squad car, well out of sight of our meeting location.

"Dang! Glad she didn't accept the ride, Magic Mike. You would have blown your own cover inviting the girl to your squad car," I kick myself as I think about Ari who has that numbing effect on me. She definitely has what it takes to make a man forget his purpose in life, and for his mind to create a new purpose of being all he can be...*for her.* "Ari," I repeat her name slowly, simply to hear it again. What a beautiful name?

Chapter Four
Ari

"Hey Sloane," I answer my buzzing phone the following night.

"Hey Ari, just checking on you. I was tied up last night and couldn't come out to back you up. Sorry about that. I hope everything went okay," he says sounding distraught.

"That's not like you, man. You're slipping," I begin, breaking Sloane's balls since he's always busting mine. "Where were you, Sloane? You call me with all of this bitching about me not letting you know when I work. Then, last night when I call you to tell you I'm about to work I don't get an answer, so who's slacking now?" I ask, playfully sarcastic.

"Sorry, I couldn't be out there last night. I was working up an arrest on the Northside, and it was sticky with an officer-involved shooting."

"Oh yeah? Who's the officer?"

"Me," he said in a grave tone, and I could have sworn I heard the faintest sniffle.

"Damn, what happened, Sloane?"

"This guy was committing an armed robbery of a gas station I just happened to be at filling up my car. When I walked into the store, I saw him waving his gun around in the back. I took out my gun and shot him because he was threatening to kill everyone in the place because they didn't have a lot of money. He wouldn't follow commands, and—" he stops midsentence and begins breathing deeply.

"Did the perp survive the shot?" I almost hated to ask.

"Yes, but someone videoed the shooting, and now it's all on social media. The higher-ups had me at headquarters all day working on the paperwork so it could be an open and closed situation when it comes to my reasoning for doing what I did." He sounds nervous as if he's not sure of himself.

"Sorry, you have to go through that. None of us want to be involved in a shooting, but it comes with the territory," I reassure him.

"You know me better than anyone else, Yan. With us both being fresh out of college and around the same age when we came into the agency years ago, we have grown together.

31

Through our talks, I have an appreciation for the plight of blacks, Latinos and other races when it comes to police shootings. You know how I feel about that. What they are saying about me is wrong. I don't deserve to be talked about as if I'm an animal, just because I was trying to save lives," he says, his voice weakening.

"Well, Sloane, I haven't even checked social media, but I do know you will guard any man, black or white, with your last breath. At the same time, you will put a bullet hole in any man involved in criminal activity and threatening the lives of others. So, if I were you, I wouldn't worry about it. Your name will be cleared in the end," I say to console him. Yet, we both know in the current polarizing state of media, and especially social media, people have already made up their minds, and there is nothing he can do to convince most of them of his true intentions. This whole situation is messed up, so I don't know what else to say to brighten his mood.

"It's easy to say not to worry about it, but man, oh, man, seeing my name go through the mud is hard. What I don't understand is how thousands of people who know nothing about me can call me a murderous pig when they don't have but a few-seconds clip of what happened."

"Well, it's the nature of the beast these days. Bad cops have made it harder for the good ones to do their jobs, that's for sure. But, don't worry about it, I'll speak up for you, Sloane. I know your heart."

"Will you do that for me, Yan?"

"Of course, I will," I tell him. "And, you're not missing much on the trafficking case either. I think they're hiding out because they've been tipped off. I haven't seen any of those girls I was suspicious of since I asked them questions about who they work for," I update Sloan.

"I was worried about you last night when I couldn't make it. That was the hardest part of the night, thinking something might happen to you while I was at the precinct filling out paperwork."

Sloane is such a protector. With all he has going on with the shooting and social media slander, he's still worried about me.

"It's okay, partner. I didn't get into much because it started raining and no one else came by. Just the guy from the other night, but it started raining before we could get to the next level."

"Good, because I worry about you. I don't know what I would do if something happens to you," he says, his voice cracking once again. Sloane doesn't have many friends in New York City. We are both implants in the city and have leaned on each other over the years.

"I know you worry, but I have been telling you since I started that just because I'm a woman doesn't mean I can't handle the men I deal with. I always think of a way to entrap them before I slap the cuffs on them. If I can't do that, there's a bullet for anyone who gets out of line," I explain.

"You definitely know how to entrap a man, and you have ways of doing it without bullets," Sloane says, his voice lowering an octave.

"Yeah, and they fall for it every time," I brag, laughing.

He laughs along with me. His laughter is a beautiful sound after the misery he's just shared with me.

"I'm at home and staying in tonight, big guy, so you don't have to worry about me. I'm going to watch Netflix until I fall asleep. Tomorrow, I'll see if I can locate those girls by talking to some of the new ones out there. They were tight-lipped at first, but after being out there a month, I think I'm gaining some of their trust."

"You're good at what you do, Ari."

"Thanks, Sloane."

"Well, enjoy your evening," he says. "I'll see you tomorrow."

"Okay. You try to enjoy your evening, too. Don't worry about what people are saying on social media. We both know you did your job, and probably saved the lives of the clerk and people in the store, too. It's what we do," I remind him.

"You're right. I feel better after talking to you."

"Good, now let me go. My movie is coming on."

"Please, let me know if you get an itch to roll out tonight. Don't go out alone. Stop trying to be a solo agent," he fusses.

"Yeah, yeah, and yeah…" I say, hanging up. *He knows me too well.*

I'm already dressed and ready to meet Blaze. I wait for him in the lobby of the motel to save him from an uncomfortable conversation with the check-in clerk at the front desk. The woman is extra chatty, and she likes to give people she thinks are my Johns a hard time.

When Blaze walks up, he's wearing comfortable looking gray sweatpants, a gray zip-up jacket, only half-zipped, with nothing on underneath, and a pair of gray LeBron tennis shoes.

Why Lord? Why must this man be so sexy with so much swag?

A sound I never heard before escapes my lips. It's instinctive, and I can't cover it up once it leaves my mouth.

"Hello," he says when he reaches me. "I hope that sound you made means you like what you see." He's charming and relaxed.

"Yes, I do like what I see," I admit, honestly. I like everything about him. Still, I will my eyes not to travel down to stare at his package. The site of it, sitting off to his right, thick and long, is calling me by my real name.

Yan-dyeee, come to the light.

"Thanks," he says, eyes narrowing even as half of his face twitches with humor. He knows I want him, and his gestures only make me want him more.

"I mean, you look…nice," I correct myself, hoping for a little more ladylikeness in this modification.

"You're looking good yourself," he commends with not only his words but the looks of lust as his eyes roam all over me in approval.

"Do you always dress like a pimp in a bad hustler movie?" I ask to break the sexual tension between us. I really am playing off the fact that everything about him is candy to my eyes.

"Only for you, Sweet Ari," he says.

All my hopes of my humor dragging me out of the spell he's bound me in, for the third night in a row, is gone.

"Big Blaze, I like you. I like you a lot," I admit.

He freezes when I call him Big Blaze as if he's startled by hearing his own name.

"Did I say something wrong?" I ask.

"Oh, nothing." He looks around, checking the mostly deserted lobby and then lowering his voice. "I just like the way you say my name. It's word porn coming from your lips."

"It's appropriate—because, you know, you're looking kind of big and blazing in those sweats. I'm just saying." If I weren't here to do a job, he is precisely the type of man to have me falling off the deep end. Who doesn't want a tall, sexy man that's fine, *and* he's packing?

He chuckles. "You're too much."

"Plus, I need a name to call you when we're…" I run my tongue over my lips to wet them and to signify what we're there to do. *Am I really about to do it? Sure seems like it.*

Blaze watches my every movement with an intense stare.

"With you looking so beautiful, it's pretty fucking easy to remember why we're here. Also, big and blazing is pretty damn accurate. So, sure, you can call me Big Blaze." He runs his hand up and down the length of what I am sure is all manhood. If he were any other John, that action would have had me ready to cuff and cart him off to jail, but the ways I want to cuff Blaze are against all the rules.

I spend the next few seconds trying to regroup from that sight alone. It's seared in my mind. How can one man be so… blessed? My mind wanders wildly. I really want to know what he's capable of doing to me in bed. That curiosity is even more pronounced since I won't get to find out.

Thoughts of Blaze moaning my name in bed leave me flush all over and burning with the desire to drag him upstairs to my 'paid for by the FBI' room and do all kinds of freaky things to him immediately. I want to kiss him more than I can remember wanting to kiss anyone. I want it all as the song goes, 'if only for one night.'

You're here to do a job! Do it, girl, and get out of this rinky-dink place. Then, go catch some more bad guys.

"Good," I say, dragging my eyes back to his cropped brown hairline and dusty brown eyes. "So, Big Blaze…" I shiver because it's even sexier hearing his name come out of my mouth that time than before. "You wanna hear what you need to do to get me upstairs to my room?" I ask, ready to trap him.

"Hell yes. Tell me what I need to do, and it's done," Blaze says in that honey-whiskey tone that has driven me mad since the first word he said to me.

"All I need is for you to pa—"

I'm cut off by the fire alarm blaring overhead; an annoying, screeching sound that makes me feel like my eardrums are going to explode.

"I'm going to fuckin' *shoot* something," he yells as all hope of us going upstairs is doused.

"I'll help," I yell back, grimly. Someone does need to get shot for causing this alarm to go off. I'm not even sure if I was just about to give in to Blaze or tease him some more, but I hate we are interrupted by this sounding alarm.

As people start to evacuate out of their rooms and out of the building, I realize this thing with Blaze and me just isn't going down. With so many things happening each time we meet, I contemplate our meeting is just not meant to be.

Blaze looks like he's more interested in helping to evacuate people out of the building than he is finding somewhere else to go, so I join him in knocking on doors and telling people they need to get out as the smell of smoke grows stronger.

Hours later, the building is evacuated, and the fire department has located and extinguished a small kitchen fire.

"You know what, I think we should just call it a night," I say, exhausted, smelling of smoke and ready to go home and lie down. At the moment, I'm tired of looking at the motel.

"No, Ari. I'd love it if we could finally get the chance to hang out. We've been at this for the third night in a row, so let's just do it. I'll go and rent a car and drive us out of the city to somewhere more secluded."

I would offer to drive my car, but I haven't had a chance to remove anything from it that might link me to the FBI, so I agree to Blaze's plan.

I yawn, the gravity of the day weighing down on me. "Sure, let's do it."

Not an hour later, Blaze pulls up to the still smoky motel building and picks me up in a blue SUV. We small talk as he jumps on the highway. At this point, I'm unsure if we're on an official date, or if I'm still just doing my job, so I go with the flow.

"So, you've only been in New York for two months?" he asks as he turns onto the expressway.

"Yeah, two months. I came up from North Carolina chasing dreams," I tell him. It's partially true. I'm living my dream of taking down bad guys, but I have been here for years.

"Oh yeah? What's your dream?" he asks.

"To be a Broadway actress," I say. It's cliché, but it also has some truth to it. When I was a little girl, I used to want to be an actress. My parents even contemplated sending me to theater school.

"I can see you doing that. You're very dramatic at times," he says. "Especially with your facial movements. You don't have a poker face."

If only he knew.

"Dramatic, oh, I can show you dramatics. If you keep shooting shots at me, I'm going to tell you about yourself," I say huffing and crossing my arms.

"That's exactly what I'm talking about. Look at how you're pouting. Broadway, look out; here she comes!" he says like an announcer for a Broadway show.

"Whatever Big Blaze," I say, and we both erupt into laughter.

Ten minutes after we get on the highway, we witness a five-car pile-up ahead of us, which backs up traffic for hours. We spend that time talking about life and what brought us both to the point we are now. I can't believe how much I tell him about myself, mostly true, as he wades through the traffic.

Opening up to him about Tracyee is especially hard, knowing he's the kind of man that keeps pimps and traffickers in business.

Five hours later, I'm convinced Blaze is just a man in need of a companion. He's not some rude and dirty trick who tries to exploit a girl's need for cash to fulfill all of his nasty desires. He's, dare I say it, a gentleman.

He pulls into a nice hotel, and we check in. We crash onto the bed as soon as we enter the room. Within minutes, we are laying in each other's arms talking about life. It's not long before the weight of the long day overtakes us and we fall asleep.

The next morning, I awake to the sound of Blaze's phone going off.

"Hey, Blaze...Blaze!" I shake him slightly as I call out his name.

"Huh?" he murmurs and sits up. "Where were we? My family is big New York Jets fans. We don't support any other team," he says groggily.

It's funny to hear him pick up where we left off talking before we fell asleep last night. We were talking about sports, and he was telling me how much his family loved the Jets before his eyes fluttered and he was asleep.

"No, your phone is ringing," I tell him, chuckling.

"Oh," he giggles then rolls over and answers it, immediately swinging his feet to the floor and hopping out of bed. "Blaze speaking... okay... no, I checked on that yesterday, and she wasn't there... Okay... Yes... No...Oh really? I'm on my way in now," he says, hangs up, and sighs.

"Is everything okay?" I ask.

"Come on, we have to go now," he says. He's still half asleep as he begins to put on his shoes.

"Do I at least have time to shower?" I ask in a pout.

He looks at me as if he's considering it. A glimmer of lust runs across his eyes, and I can see them undressing me and carrying me into the shower.

"A shower… that would be nice, and it's so tempting, but I have an emergency. I have to go now," he says sternly.

"Okay." I get up and start putting on my shoes, as well.

When we reach the door of the hotel, Blaze turns to me and pulls me into his arms. With a ragged sigh, he pushes strands of my hair out of my face.

"I had an amazing night with you, Ari. It was better than anything we could have done sexually. I enjoyed just talking to you. It was really nice."

I nearly dissolve in his arms. My heart is raging out of my chest. I feel like melting in this man's arms over the way he's looking at me. He doesn't just say good things; he looks at me like he means every single word. Why does he have to be someone who picks up prostitutes?

"I had a great time, too," I say, and his lips meet mine before the last word is spoken.

I freeze for a second, trying to halt the feelings I know are coming next. The comfort. The desire. The heat. He is so different than any other man that has tried to pick me up, and it's easy to feel something for him.

"Let's do this again tonight," he says, pulling back to look into my eyes. "Minus the rain or fire, of course."

"Don't forget the screaming old lady," I say with a chuckle.

"How could I forget her?" he laughs along with me. "I'll see you tonight then?"

"Yes."

"Great. I'll come by after I get off work," he says. He takes my hand and leads me out of the hotel hand in hand. The entire time my hand is in his, I feel as though I'm on fire...a blazing fire. I can't wait until nightfall.

Chapter Five
Blaze

I drop Ari back off at the motel and very pointedly analyze the fact that moments ago I felt so comfortable lying in bed with a suspected criminal. Sure, I spent most of last night stuck in traffic with her, talking about everything from when I was a young boy playing tee ball to my football days in college. Granted, she and I are so compatible, from our zest for life to our tarnished dreams, it's easy to talk to her because she understands me. And that kiss. It took every bone in my body to pull me away from her lips. If the chief hadn't called me, I'd still be drinking from her lips.

I miss her already, but she told me her room number, and I'll be getting back to see her as soon as I can. At the moment, I have to go to the station to lend my hand to a cold case. Someone just called in a tip to the tip line. Had that call not come, I would have taken Ari up on that shower, and we would be rocking each other to ecstasy at this very moment. I have no doubts about that. Yeah, this so-called undercover sting has gone far beyond an officer looking for his next perp. I'm a goner.

I pull up to the station and immediately retrain my thoughts. It's Monday morning, so hopefully, with the new week to come, I'll get my head back in the game. I have a lot of cases to solve, a community to serve, and egos to stroke at city hall. Nowhere on my schedule is there time to fall in love.

My day is grueling, and the chief sends me all over town chasing tips. After a long day, I head home. I've already put in a full twelve hours looking for a missing young lady who we believe fell prey to the underground sex trafficking networks of NYC, so I'm taking the evening off to recharge.

The thought crosses my mind to go to Ari's as I promised, but I fight it off, opting to eat, shower and lie down. I told her I would see her again tonight, but after I spend the day in cop mode, I have rearranged my thoughts and put my priorities in order. Her lifestyle is part of a bigger problem I work every day to fix. I can't get my head clouded with feelings of love and lust. It will only hamper my ability to help others.

As soon as sleep assails me, dreams of Ari live on Broadway dancing and singing her heart out in a majestic type of stage play fill my head. The one recurring thing in this dream is her beautiful smile.

The next two nights are filled with the same—dreams about Ari. The dreams are enough to keep me satisfied. I'm not going to call her or try to see her ever again. I'm going to go about bringing these traffickers to justice another way that doesn't involve her arrest. At least, those are the lines I feed myself.

By Thursday night, I can't take it anymore. I have to see her. I'm standing in front of her motel room door, knocking, but no one answers. I go back to the park and then the alley where I first spotted her.

There she is in the alley, standing with her back pressed to the old stone wall and one foot propped up on an old stump for support. This woman has a stance like no other. Once again, I know it's her by the nasty way she's standing there watching me approach her.

As soon as I reach her, the lust, the feeling of love, the dreams, everything I've been feeling for her this past week erupts into an embrace, and my lips come crashing down on hers. It feels like heaven as we connect, my hands steadily moving up her thigh while I suck her tongue for its nectar.

The kiss gets increasingly heated. Ari climbs the wall as if she's trying to get away from me yet come to me at once. I make a guttural sound at the sensation of my cock brushing against her womanhood. I tighten my grip on Ari's hips so that I won't try to rip off her clothes right there in the alley. At least, I have that tiny bit of control left.

Hey!" a familiar voice shouts, from an open window behind us, sounding furious. "How many times do I have to tell you two that this is private property! Be gone in five seconds, or I'm calling the cops. One— two—" the woman begins counting.

"Hold your horses, lady. We're leaving!" I say and grab Ari's hand. This time, I'm prepared. I didn't come in my squad car. I drove a rental, ready to usher her to the nearest hotel and have my way with her.

"Can we stop for coffee?" she asks. It's an unusual request, especially after the sexual tension we just shared, but her wish is my command.

"Sure. Anything you want," I tell her, knowing she's stalling and prolonging the inevitable. We are made for the love we are about to share, and she's worth the wait.

I glance at Ari every chance I can as I ride as fast as I can toward the closest Starbucks. I have so many questions about her that need answers.

Why does she need to have sex for money? Does she have a terminally ill grandmother? Are her student loans that expensive? Does she have a brother she needs to pay bail to get out of prison? Is she planning to pay someone off at Broadway so she can get a role? The wilder the reasons I come up with, the less I can bring myself to pull out my badge. If she's suffering through something tragic, she doesn't deserve to have an arrest heaped on top of her.

Plus, she's far too pretty to go to jail. People will do terrible things to her on the inside. The only person who should be allowed to do terrible things to Ari is me. Which brings me to the question I

51

desire to know the answer to the most: *How wet and warm can she get for me?*

We make it to Starbucks, place our orders and wait for our drinks. I gaze across the room of plush sofas and arresting Ari is the furthest thing from my mind. Because of her, I have a whole new morning jerk-off routine, considering how often I'm woken up from dreams about finally getting to see her pretty pussy and needing to take care of myself. I'm on the verge of going insane, only a few moments away from taking my gun to the shooting range and firing away all of the fucking sexual tension that's keeping me up at night.

Thankfully, Ari's wearing something that's not causing all of my blood to rush south, for once. She's wearing an oversized, pink shirt, loose black jeans, and flats. She looks as good in modest clothing as she does in her late night 'uniforms.' Her hair is tamer, slicked to the back with something. There's a black and pink scarf around her neck with a broach that makes her look regal.

"Blaze!" the barista calls our order, and I hop up to get it.

I put Ari's coffee thermos on the table so that she can tear a pack of sugar with her teeth and drop it into her drink. I am ridiculously charmed by that little detail; the fact that she cares enough about the environment to carry her own thermos in her purse. Ari looks and acts like someone I can *have;* someone I can take home and introduce to my mom. The whole scene makes my breath catch.

"I need to get some more creamer," I say to excuse myself from her mesmerizing innocent beauty. I walk over to the condiment station and give my hardness a moment to go down before returning.

I stare at Ari as I walk back to the table. Her eyes go wide with recognition of my attention to her, a breathtaking shade of hazel. Coffee mug forgotten beside her elbow, Ari tugs her bottom lip between her teeth in a self-conscious motion that goes straight to my dick.

My feet carry me across the room on autopilot. I'm a piece of scrap metal, drawn irresistibly to a magnet. Ari helps to close the distance, coming around the table. In only a few seconds, she is in arm's reach.

"My apartment is a one-minute walk away," I tell her, breathing a little harder in anticipation. It's what we both want, and apparently, from the twinkle in her hazel eyes, it's what we both need. "There was no construction; no rain; no fires; no traffic jams; nothing at all wrong ten minutes ago when we drove over here. So, I can't think of anything that would get in our way tonight. *Please* come home with me."

Ari is breathing hard, chest rising and falling in time with mine, and lips bitten red. "Yes," she says, fervently.

I take her by the hand, and we walk out the door into the parking lot. I turn and grab her by the waist, pulling her body against mine. My fingers slip into her curly hair as I plant my mouth on hers again. The taste of her lips is so good to me. I can't wait to have her pinned between my body and the wall.

She returns the kiss, giving herself to me freely. For a split second, I wonder if this is something she does for all men, or if it's something special she has for me. We kiss until she convinces me it's something special, made just for this moment we're sharing. A moan escapes from deep within my throat when she licks my lips as part of the most sensual kiss I've ever received.

I take her hand and guide her around to the passenger's side to let her into the car before running around to the driver's seat, cranking up and getting to my apartment in record speed.

Chapter Six
Ari

The very moment we get inside Blaze's apartment, he pushes me back against the wall and kisses me hard, much harder than before. This time, there's immeasurable passion flowing from him. Hands clenched in my scarf, as he handles me roughly, he shows me he's not the gentle giant I think he is.

We taste like the coffee we abandoned back in the store, thermos and all.

He looks incredible, curls windswept and cheeks pink from the cold weather. He kisses back with equal fervor like he's been wanting this as much as I have. That's gratifying. It's terrific to feel wanted, and every conscious part of me tells me these are his true feelings.

When his neck bends as far as possible—he's much taller than me—he lifts me in one push, using the leverage of the wall. I go with it, wrapping my legs around Blaze's waist and hooking my arms around the back of his head. In that position, it's all too easy for him to press into my body and keep me there, his manhood brushing against my womanhood every time one of us dives back into the kiss.

"Fuck, Blaze," I murmur. "Holy fuck, you're so fucking hot. Your fucking *arms*…" F-bombs come out of my mouth with ease until my words drop off as my hands roam his muscular arms. *Are so fucking big and strong…* I complete the thought in my head for fear his python-like arms will squeeze the life out of me if I say it aloud. He's taking over every part of me, especially my mind, and I'm allowing it. "I love being in your arms," I admit.

"I love having you in them, Ari. You're so sexy." He scrapes his teeth along the underside of my jaw. "I've been thinking about you for *weeks*," he admits. Blaze is rumpled-looking as he wildly caresses me, and he sounds like his ability to control himself is completely lost.

My control is fraying more with every kiss we share. I fit perfectly in his arms, like the second half of a puzzle piece. I want to take advantage of that, want to erase every other woman he's ever held from his mind. Even if after tonight he never calls me again, I'm determined to be the best fuck he's ever had.

"You're gorgeous," he continues. "Ari, *God*, your mouth. I want your lips on my cock. I want to see my cum on your tongue. I want to see you take it all in your mouth," he says.

I yank his pants and briefs down, and he immediately stops talking. The knowledge of what's about to happen has his eyes glazed over with delight. My eyes equally glaze over when his big, rock-hard cock flings out as if it's a third arm. My mouth waters at the sight of its beauty.

"Everything about you is sexy," I say to him as I open my mouth and begin licking the head of his beautiful dick. I lick down to the shaft and back up before I take him all in, a ritual I repeat until my name is bouncing off his apartment walls. After teasing him this way for a while, I take him all the way to the back of my throat, while staring up at him.

His widened eyes indicate he is impressed. As I take him from the roof of my mouth to the depths of my throat, I make a tight gap with my lips, teasing the head with my tongue and moving it along the vast expanse of his cock. I take him in and out, over and over until he can't help but to growl like an animal, grab the back of my head, and grind as if he's fucking my pussy. That's what I want, his groans of pleasure to be seared into my mind—a sound so sweet.

I don't know what turns me on more, hearing his sex sounds or giving him head. I create a rhythm with him that elicits more of those sounds I love so much. Blaze closes his eyes, showing his enjoyment of my soft, wet mouth devouring his cock with each thrust. When his balls tighten, I can taste the fruits of my labor trickling down my throat. I want it, and I want it all. He grunts and calls out my name as his strokes intensify with the extreme pleasure I know is building inside of him.

"Ari, baby. I'm coming." He tries to pull back so that he won't come in my mouth, but I latch onto his thighs and savagely pull him deep into my throat as his hot seed spills inside of me.

As I said, I want it all.

Blaze's explosive orgasm tastes just as delicious as I believed it would. I look up at him with a grin, swallowing my treats, and he looks at me, amazed.

"Whoa! What was that?" Blaze says, ribs constricting. He looks like he is having an out of body experience as his body continues to jerk and recoil from the sweetest tasting blow job I've ever given.

I giggle. "We're just getting started, Big Blaze."

"Oh shit, tonight is going to be wonderful. It's the best night of my life already," he says smiling. "Let's take this to the bedroom."

Blaze walks me down the hallway and into his bedroom. Once inside, he turns on the light and starts to make up his bed. I open my mouth to say something about helping him, and the doorbell rings, bringing our attention to it.

"Are you expecting someone?" I ask.

"No. Whoever it is, I'm going to tell them to get lost, so make yourself comfortable on the bed, and I'll be right back," he says, kissing me again.

"Okay," I agree and sit on the edge of his bed. There isn't much furniture, just the bed and a dresser, but his room is tidy.

I hear Blaze pad back up the hall and open the door.

"Hey, man. What's up?" he asks whoever is on the other side.

"Nothing, just stopping by to get my clothes. What are you doing? You look like you just ran a marathon or something," a man's voice asks.

"No marathon, bro, but I am busy. I'll get your clothes for you. Hold on," Blaze returns to the room and grabs an outfit out the closet. It's on hangers and wrapped in a clear bag. "Be back in just a second, baby," he says, pecking my lips once more before he trots back up the hall.

"Here you go, Terry," Blaze says, and I surmise Terry is a good friend of his from the way they are talking.

"Thanks, man. Are you watching that game that's on now? It looks like our team is about to lose," I hear Terry say. "Turn to it; it should be in the fourth quarter," he adds.

"No, I'm not watching the game. I have better things to do with my time, tonight," Blaze indicates, and the hint is obvious. "How about we catch up later?" he asks.

"Oh, I see. You got a woman back there. Is she fine?" Terry asks.

"What kind of question is that? You know she's fine if she's here with me," Blaze says sounding cocky.

"That's right. What was I thinking?" Terry asks, and then giggles as if his question is meant to be sarcasm. "You and that hooker from the other night didn't get any jizz on my clothes, did you?" Terry's trying to whisper, but I hear him.

I'm already eavesdropping, but that statement causes me to listen more intently. I get up and start walking toward the living room.

"I told you I wouldn't get anything on your clothes, man."

The front door creaks open. I step into the room to see Blaze running his fingers through his hair with one hand while holding the door open for his friend to exit with the other.

"Hi," Blaze's friend says to me, then turns to Blaze. "Wow, I can see why you're putting me out. She is super sexy! Is this the girl you borrowed the suit for?" he asks.

"Are you trying to ask if I'm the whore he's sleeping with for money?" I cut to the chase. I don't like people that beat around the bush with their insults, so Terry rubs me the wrong way from the get-go. "If you're trying to insult me, just come right out with it, why don't you?"

"No, I didn't mean it that wa—"

"Later, man." The sound of Blaze's voice lets me know he's frustrated his friend is messing up our night. "I'll catch you some other time," he adds with a frown.

"Alright man, you don't have to tell me three times. Have fun tonight," Terry says, and I can hear the smirk in his tone. That along with the way he looks at me like I'm the trick for hire that I pretend to be.

Blaze closes the door without saying anything else to him.

"So, do you go out and hunt for prostitutes often while wearing your friend's clothes, or was I your first? Please tell me I'm your first, so I can at least feel special in some way." I don't mean to sound hurt, or even upset, but I sound like a wounded animal when I ask that question.

"Ari," he begins, and a pang from my own dishonesty of not giving him my real name shoots through me. I push it back because I'm the only one that should be in their feelings at this very moment. "Let me explain," he says.

I walk over to stand closer to him. "I'm listening."

Chapter Seven
Blaze

When Terry asks if 'the hooker got jizz on his clothes,' I know I'm in trouble. My apartment is only so big that I'm sure loud-mouth Terry's voice resonates throughout it. I try to get him out as quickly as he comes in, but he can't catch a clue to save his life. When Ari walks into the room, and my eyes land on hers, the almost imperceptible flinch in her face grips me. If I wasn't trained to conduct interrogations, I might've missed it, but with all the experience I've had, it might as well be a blinking neon light that Terry has crossed a line. *This is why I shouldn't be on this assignment!* I lament silently.

I'm so far from capable of dealing with beautiful prostitutes that literally anyone else in the entire precinct could have done a better job than I'm doing right now. The fact that I'm starting to think I'll be okay with getting fired if I can only get an orgasm out of Ari is a clear sign of my incompetence.

"He let me borrow an outfit the other night."

"Yeah, but my question is do you usually play dress up when you're looking for prostitutes, Blaze?" She crosses her arms over her chest and waits for me to answer. I don't like hearing the hurt in her voice.

Damn you, Terry. Your big ass mouth is always running.

"Baby, listen to me." I pull her close to me. "I don't usually go looking for prostitutes," I admit truthfully. "My friend can be a talkative asshole, but that's him. Tell me, did *I* say or do something to offend you?"

"No, it wasn't anything you said."

"And, I never would say or do anything to offend you, Ari. Not knowingly anyway. So, don't let what someone else does affect us, okay?"

"I don't know what I'm feeling right now. This is just a very complicated situation," she admits as she pulls away from me.

And I don't know what I'm feeling either. Except I know what I want to touch, feel, and experience, and it isn't an argument.

"You'll have to tell me your boundaries. If you don't want me to open the door or answer the phone when you're around, it's done," I submit.

"You didn't do anything wrong, per se. It's just—"

"What is it, baby?"

"Nothing."

"I did say something wrong, didn't I?" I can't explain why I'm so concerned about her feelings. I haven't cared about what a woman thought this deeply in…forever. "Tell me what it is and I'll fix it. It will never happen again."

"I just got offended with him insinuating I'm just some prostitute as if I don't mean anything to—" She catches herself before she finishes that thought. "Well, we're only here for the moment, I suppose," she says instead.

Ari studies me and comes to stand close to me once again. My arms envelop her, and I pick her up.

"Ari, you just don't know—" I stop talking as her legs wrap around me, and the heat from her body warms me all over. She rocks her hips in slow, lazy motions. She starts to smile when I can't hold back a grunt at the spark that friction causes. I get momentarily mesmerized watching as Ari's pupils go from a light hazel to a darker shade of brown.

"We're just two strangers enjoying a moment, right?" she asks.

"Oh, baby," is all I can muster from the feel of her womanhood pressing against my cock. All I know in this moment is I want this woman more than my next breath. "I want you," I groan against her ear.

"If tonight is all we have, promise me one thing," she says.

"Anything."

"Please, let's take it slow."

"I just want to make you happy for as long as I can, Ari," I mutter against her ear.

"I'll sort out my feelings tomorrow. But, I can assure you, *Blaze*, everything you're doing is making me happy."

"You promise?" I pant, holding back from another kiss.

Ari rolls her eyes but looks pleased. "I *promise,* Prince Charming."

Fuck, I can feel the heat radiating off her pussy, and I want my dick inside of it so badly. I cave and cover her lips with mine. Even though I know I'm being made fun of, I don't care.

Feeling Ari's hands drop to the buttons of my jeans, I suck in my stomach, helpfully, giving Ari more room to free my cock from my boxers at once. I take a hand off the wall and slide it up Ari's stomach under her shirt, feeling nothing but a smooth softness. Apparently, being in her profession calls for a lot of gym time because her body is a work of art.

In the corner of my eye, I catch sight of my badge sitting face up on a side table, taunting me. Ari grabs my face and pulls me in for a particularly heated stretch of kisses where she starts to stroke the shaft of my cock with her soft fingers. Fuck, fuck, fuck. This isn't what I'm supposed to be doing. That damn badge is a reminder that if I don't have the stomach to arrest Ari, I should at least tell her the truth and give her the chance to get away.

"Wait," I gasp, arching up on my toes.

Ari presses her thumb into the head of my dick, dragging a string of strange sounds out of me.

"But..." I groan, trying to bat Ari's hand away. "We haven't agreed on... you know–" I trail off, too distracted to care about what I need to be saying to her. Ari has unzipped my jeans enough to start to work my shaft in earnest, and my life is literally in her hands.

"I don't care about that," Ari says, her legs in a vice-like clamp around my ass. "I just want to taste you again. Do whatever; buy me takeout or something," she purrs out.

I barely hear her statement. Instead, I'm about to come all over my pants. "Whatever you want," I say, yanking at Ari's scarf and throwing it off to the side. "It's yours."

Ari taps me lightly on the shoulder so I will put her down. She drops to her knees right there in the foyer and gives me the second most spectacular blow-job I ever had in my life, second only to her earlier performance. Sucking lightly on my balls, while her wrist works from head to base, it's so good I almost manage to entirely suppress the stab of jealousy I feel thinking about *how* Ari got to be so good.

I insist on returning the favor. Even though it's probably not how Ari's transactions usually go, the guilt of partaking of her glorious lips twice in one night has me ready to eat her from her stomach to her ass and back again. She doesn't put up much of a fight.

Once I have climaxed, leaving my seed deep within Ari's throat, I switch us around, snatch off her bottoms and spread her legs. She braces for me as I nestle between her thighs, taking time to inhale her fragrant cunt. It smells so good that I'm ready to dive in, never to be seen or heard from again. The way her pussy looks, brown with pink goodness inside has to be a picture of the promised land.

I open her legs wider and slide my tongue into her slit, playing with her clit. She's so wet that it's not long before another wave of juices gush from her cove and coat my tongue with deliciousness. Her taste and the sound of her moans are enough to drive a sane man wild. I grip her thighs, holding her in place so that I can move deeper inside her. I want to drink up everything she has to offer, pulling juices from her wells deep within.

"Blaze!" she calls out, squirming as I tighten my grip on her.

"Yes, baby," I murmur against her lower lips. "You like that, Ari?"

"Yes!" she howls into the night, and I can see her eyes spacing out, and her legs start shaking and getting weak.

My muscles flex as I hold her up. Knowing she's about to come undone adds to the pleasure. My tongue strikes her tasty button deep with precision, and involuntary jerks racking through her body reward me. It's a rippling effect because, after a few moments, I'm painting circles of passion on her pussy and about to make her lose it again. I pleasure her going clockwise until she's used to it. Then, I switch it up and go the other way. It's a level of insanity I love experiencing with her; this experience is driving us both insane.

Her moans and groans turn into full-fledged growls. She starts to orgasm, shaking and trying to squirm away from me.

"Blaze, I can't—take it!" she calls out, as her juices rush forth coating my tongue like a waterfall.

I don't stop drinking from her, digging deep to extract every drop, until she falls limp into my arms. Then, I pick her up and take her to my bedroom. I place her on the bed and immediately strip out of my clothes.

Ari lay on the bed too limp to do anything, so I remove the rest of her clothes also. I know what she wants, what she needs, and I've just begun. Her body comes alive when she sees me rolling on a condom. I get several steps away from the bed before she finds her strength to scoot up to the center of the bed.

"Will you be gentle with me?" she asks, staring at my swollen cock.

Something about the way she asks me to be gentle shakes me to my core.

"If that's what you want," I say in a full tone coated with desire, especially after her change in tone from nasty girl to someone I could love slow and gently, dare I say forever.

I flop onto my back, pulling her down on top of me and opting to let her have her way. She moans so sweetly as she kisses me passionately. I'm hungry for her. I crave for the moment her heat covers my shaft more than I crave anything in life. I can take the tease no longer. I have to get inside of her. I grip her ass cheeks, lift her and guide her down onto my length slowly.

Ari cries out my name as she takes me all in. She begins to ride me at her own rhythm, and the slow grind of her hips is exhilarating. At this rhythm, which I'm sure is made only for us, I know I'll be cumming in no time.

I grip her perky breasts to pull my attention from the way she is milking the cum out of my cock. I lean forward and take one nipple into my mouth, sucking it to inflict pain as she rides me. Her slick vagina is intoxicating enough, but the taste of her brown pebble in my mouth is mind-blowing.

I imagine how the sheen of moisture without barriers would feel as she begins to slide up and down my shaft in a slow, grinding motion. Ari's mouth hangs open in an O as she looks down at me, eyes hooded over. She looks as if I'm giving her the best pleasure she's ever had when I'm the one who's hanging on by a thread. I grab her ass, clutching it in my fingers to take control. If she continues to move in her seductive rhythm, I will not last long enough to do the things I want to do to her.

Ari bounces up and down on my cock, and the pleasure of her riding builds with every single bounce. Her pussy is raining like water down onto my thighs and soaking the sheets. I am so deep inside of her; it feels like I'll come out on the other side. I love how she's able to take all of me, my length going deeper inside with each bounce.

We moan together, groan together, and growl like two animals rutting. Our cries bounce off the walls. At no moment do I feel like a man paying for a service. It feels like this is a connection of lovers, something that's meant to be, finally.

I lean forward and wrap my arms around her, then roll over landing on top of her. Her soft, pliable skin contours to my body as I lay on top of her. The way I'm about to make love to her is something that should be off limits with any woman I'm not seriously dating, much less someone I'm supposed to arrest, but I kiss her, sliding my tongue into her mouth as I ease back into her slick vagina. Laying directly on her, I kiss every spot I can reach while I take her deeply and slowly.

Her moans never stop coming, and I feel as though I'm going to burst from the sound alone. Ari begins to meet my thrusts, and our bodies collide with passionate force, forcing our genitals to lock together tighter each time.

Now, it's me calling out her name, as she pulls my ass into her. I wrap my arms around her waist to pound into her deeper. A burning sensation builds in my chest, and a tingle builds in my balls, letting me know this is going to be the best one yet. This climax rages through me, ready to erupt.

"You're so hot," I say as my hot seed fills the barrier between us. I mean it, too. She is heated inside and out.

She screams in pleasure, her warm juices coating the latex. Considering how flush Ari's brown cheeks get when she's close to coming, how rich the sounds are, spilling from her lips, I don't understand why the first man that saw her on the streets didn't make an honest woman out of her already.

"Do you want me to go?" she asks with uncertainty in her voice, as I'm still spinning from the power and beauty of making love to her.

"No. Why would you think that?" I want Ari to never, ever, leave my apartment again. If only I could put her in cuffs for *that,* or even for other bed-related activities.

"I just thought I'd ask because, I don't know…" her voice trails off.

"Baby, I want you to stay with me," I admit. "Besides, you can't leave because I owe you takeout. You should hang out with me tonight. Spend the night; it's not like we have to be shy around each other anymore."

"Uh…," Ari says, seeming to do some kind of mental calculation before she gives up entirely, shrugging. "Okay. That sounds good."

I get up and get my cell out of the living room, taking the time to stuff my badge under a pile of mail. When I come back into the bedroom, Ari is already sleeping. I take a moment to gaze upon her beauty. And man is she good-looking while lying in the center of my bed with my brown sheets wrapped around her body.

I place the order for takeout, in case she wakes up hungry. Then, I climb in bed beside her and pull her to me. She fits so perfectly into my grooves that I don't see why I can't keep her forever.

"I really should go," she mumbles before dozing off again.

"Sleep beautiful," I whisper into her ear. I kiss her shoulder blades and hold her in my arms, cherishing whatever time I have left with her.

***

An hour later, her eyes flutter open. "What time is it?"

"After eleven. Do you have somewhere to go?" I ask her.

"No, but I should go home."

"Just stay here, and I'll get you home early in the morning."

"Well, I have a little work to do tonight. I really should go. I should already have been there by now," she admits.

That admission deflates my mood. Seeing her slide out of my bed and into her clothes does something to me, something it should not be doing.

"Do you *have* to go? Can it wait until tomorrow?" I ask as she walks out of my room with me following behind her closely.

"No, it's something big I'm working on. I had planned not to work tonight, but I just remembered I have something I need to do," she says, eyes averted from mine.

"You've already worked on something big," I tease. Though I'm not really in the joking mood, I want her to stay. I don't want another man to touch what feels like in my heart should be all mine.

"Funny, not funny, Blaze," she says, poking my naked chest with her finger.

"Keep poking the bear, and I'll poke back," I tease. I know for sure I'm a goner now. She's bringing the silliness out of me.

"I bet you will. That's why I have to go now," she says and giggles before her eyes land on the kitchen table. "Oh, you ordered the takeout?"

"It came thirty minutes ago, but you were sleeping so good that I didn't want to wake you up."

She walks over to the bag and inhales. "I'm hungry."

"We did work up an appetite, but I didn't want to eat without you."

"Awe, well, get some plates and let's eat."

"I think they put some in here," I say, opening the bag. "Yeah, everything we need is in here, so allow me to serve you Miss Ari...what's your last name?"

"Martin."

"Well, allow me to serve you, Miss Ari Martin."

I'm glad she has at least agreed to stay and have dinner with me. It's a midnight dinner, but dinner nonetheless.

"You're such the gentleman, Blaze." She giggles and sits down at the table. "Now, hurry up, I'm starving. The least you can do is feed a girl."

"You're right; it's the least I can do. But it's not all I want to do."

"What do you want to do?" she asks curiously.

"I want to give you everything I have to give."

"Oh, wow! That's a lot to give some prostitute that you've only known a short time. What's it been a little over a week, maybe two weeks?"

"You're not just some prostitute, Ari. You're a woman with a good sense of humor, you're kind with the right amount of sass, and you're passionate. I haven't spent a lot of time around you, but in the time we have spent together you have shown me the wonderful parts of you that

I don't want to let go. I also can look into your eyes and know all of these things are true about you, and I want more of it."

"Why are you saying all of this to me? I've never had anyone talk to me the way you do, Blaze. But let's be real, it hasn't been that long ago since you were out surfing for random women to take home."

Dang. How do I come back from that?

I could tell her the truth and let the pieces fall where they may. But, that would be reckless and could end with her storming out and never coming back.

"I was lonely," I admit, which is the truth. I didn't have anyone to call my own. Before I went out on this assignment and met her, the only thing I had to keep me company was my work and calls home to Mom. "Seeking out women for hire isn't something I normally do or agree with. I just found myself out there that night searching for something. Then I saw you, and I was drawn to you," I say truthfully. Everything I'm saying is one hundred percent truth with a few omissions.

"I'm curious. Since you don't normally find women this way or agree with it, what are your thoughts on me being out there?" she asks.

"I want you to quit," I say without hesitation. "I want you here with me. I can show you much better things in life if you let me."

She pushes her half-eaten plate away from her. "I have to go."

"We were having such a good conversation. Why leave now?"

"We can get together again tomorrow," she says, avoiding my question as she stands to her feet.

"I hate that you're leaving, but I would be happy to see you again tomorrow, Ari. Do you want me to come to pick you up?" I ask, trying very hard not to think about where Ari has to run off to. Every conclusion leaves me upset that another man might touch her tonight. But if it's one thing I'm confident about, it's knowing he won't be able to touch her as deeply as I have already.

"No, I'll come to you around ten," she promises.

I kiss her for a long time at the door, making sure to slip the takeout receipt—with my number carefully written out on the back—into her back pocket. I want her to be able to reach me at all times. I walk her to her car and come back to my apartment and plop down on the sofa.

I slowly feel myself opening up the vaults of things that should be locked away from a woman like Ari—a nightwalker that dwells in places of criminality and dishonesty. None of how I feel about her makes sense, but I can't stop this feeling, not even if I want to.

***

It keeps happening, over and over again. I'll send her a text around ten or eleven at night, trying to work around her schedule, and she keeps coming over, somehow always miraculously in between clients. Sometimes, I can't find it in myself to sleep with her due to the jealousy that sparks in my mind just at the thought of other men touching her.

I like Ari. She's hilarious, smart as hell, good in bed, and ridiculously hot, whether she's dressed regally or wearing a 'come fuck me dress' designed to make married men spend all their money on sex.

I can't bring myself to ruin Ari's life by arresting her. I've written it off at work, passing the assignment off to someone else, and hoping they go in another direction, to any other hooker in the entire city besides Ari. I have reserved myself to the fact that I'm going to continue 'paying' Ari for sex with meals and spending time with her. I hope to fucking hell that no one in the department ever finds out about us. That will be the end of my career as a police officer, and as of right now at thirty-six years old I have thirty years left before retirement. I laugh at that thought.

Except, the thing is, I'm not sure I've actually *paid* Ari for sex; not in a way that counts. We've fallen into this weird bartering pattern, just shy of illegal. I've made passionate love to her in every way imaginable—oral sex, sex in the car, sex in public, sex hard and fast, sex slow and sensually. But the barter is always, "Order some Thai," or "…grab me a bottle of wine before I get there."

The first time Ari slept over the entire night, accidentally falling asleep after I pounded her until tears were leaking out of the corners of her eyes. I had been nervous that was going to be the straw that broke the camel's back—that for some reason Ari was going to turn around and demand compensation for all the other meetings she'd missed that night. Instead, she only smiled at me across the pillows, half of her face illuminated by a beam of sun coming in through a window.

"Do you have pancake mix?" she'd asked me the next morning and even helped me flip them.

It's risky and unexplainable what Ari and I share. Something in my gut tells me she's not who I think she is. She's too good to be out in the streets working. But, she continues to slip away from me whenever I'm sleeping. I wake up to an empty bed, ready to chase after her…to pursue the next feeling of passion we will undoubtedly share. Whatever this is between us, I don't want it to end.

Chapter Eight
Ari

"Are you okay, Ari? You haven't been working all week. Our arrests have gone down the tank. We've only arrested ten men this month, and we only have a few days left. That's a long way from the thirty-six men we took down last month. We were averaging at least one perp a day then. How are we going to explain this slump to our boss? It's not like the men aren't out here picking up women," my partner, Sloane, stands in front of me at the park trying to figure out where my head is.

"I know, it's just been a slow month for me," I say dismissively.

I haven't had the desire to pretend to want to take men home since I met Blaze. Doing that means I have to transfer sexual energy to them, allow them to talk to me any kind of way, allow them to touch me, and I don't want that anymore.

"Slow month, eh?"

"That's what I said. Slow, Sloane. Now, get off my back!" Sloane is the type of person I have to ward off before he gets started. If I don't get sassy with him at the start of our conversation, I'll be listening to him talk smack for hours.

"Well, it's going to be slow if we're not working, and by we, I mean *you* because I can't go in the room with these men."

"Well, technically, you could," I remind him. "Some of them are looking for that kind of action."

"You're getting off the point, Yan. There's no way you're going to convince me that no one's tricking just because it's December. I see transactions that appear to be happening with the other girls out here, but I have no insight on what's going on because my partner is out of commission," he argues.

Sloane knows as well as I do these men will come out here and trick if it's the last thing they do. Even if there is a fifty-fifty chance the gates of hell will open up and suck them in on the spot, they'll take that chance. Hell, some of them might even think it's kinky.

"I'm here now, okay," I say, not caring enough to offer an excuse for not working. My time with Blaze is off limits for this discussion.

"Well, I went by your house, and you weren't there. You weren't at any of your usual spots. What's going on with you lately? You've never slacked on the job, so it has to be something."

"Stop being so pushy and nosey, Sloane. I just needed some time for myself. Am I allowed that?" I ask.

One of the guys I suspect of beating up a prostitute last week walks in front of us. He's headed over to where there is a group of girls, so I think quick.

"Go on about your business if you don't want to pay the forty dollars!" I yell at Sloane, giving him the nod, so he'll know I'm going back undercover. "I'm not fucking with you for free!" I tell Sloane.

"That's right. You heard the lady," the man turns on his heels to say. He's a big, husky man, and his skin is blistering red from the cold air. He should be at home somewhere trying to stay warm, but he's always out here soliciting women so he can brutalize them in a nearby motel.

Sloane slinks away. "My bad, big guy. You can take this one because I'm just not paying that much. It's out of my price range," he says before disappearing.

"So, what are you looking for tonight, big money?" I ask the man.

He coughs, and it sounds horrible. "A good time is what I want," he begins. "Can you give it to me without any attitude? These other girls don't know how to treat a man, but they want to take a man's money," he says, his voice coming out raspy and weak sounding.

I itch to reach inside my bag and pull out my gun. Any wrong move and I'm shooting him where he stands.

"No attitude here. Just all performance. I can do whatever you want," I say to the man who's about to hack up a lung. My stomach cringes at the thought of going anywhere alone with him.

"That's what I like to hear. See, you sound professional. What are you asking for?"

"Forty for blow jobs and a hundred for everything, head, and penetration," I say, my stomach curling more.

"Shit, as fine as you are baby, I want everything. How much for me to get in that pretty, round ass of yours? Ooouu, I bet it's tight too." His fat tongue slides out of his mouth, and he licks his lips.

My stomach lurches. I don't like this guy.

"To have anal with everything else, it'll be one fifty."

"Oh girl, I can't wait to get you back to my room. Come on; we can get in my car back here. I'll drive us to the motel; it's the one right around the corner." He coughs that horrid cough again and hocks a big wad of spit onto the pavement. Then, he walks off with more pep in his step than he had before.

I start to walk behind him while reaching inside my purse. This is a signal to Sloane that I'm ready to arrest the guy. I follow the man to where his car is parked as I watch Sloane move in close to us. Just as the man reaches for the door of his vehicle to let me in, I produce my gun with the safety released.

"It's always something with you women. What are you doing, lady?" he asks, his voice going high as a soprano note.

"You are under arrest for soliciting a prostitute. Anything you say or do can, and will, be used against you in a court of law. You have a right to speak to an attorney, and to have one represent—"

"I'm not going to jail. Who's going to make me, you?" he asks then lunges toward me.

"Put your hands up!" I yell, bringing my gun into full view. "Or, your brain matter will be an official part of the pavement. Give me one reason and the people of New York City will trample over your remains like you've been trampling over these women out here."

"I can't stand you damn whores! Always think you're better than us men, just because we're paying. Anyone I trampled deserved it."

"Just like you deserve this trip to the jail," Sloane says. He has sneaked the man and placed him in his grip from behind. "Now, you do what Agent Martin instructed you to do the easy way, or we can do this the hard way, which as you can see has already begun."

The man starts coughing as Sloane holds his hands behind his back. He immediately stops resisting and agrees to be cuffed. But, just when he's lowering his hands, he reaches behind his back into his waistband.

Sloane is screaming orders at him, and I have a split second to react. I shoot him in the kneecap, bringing him down to the ground. Sloane quickly cuffs him, and we get medics on the way. Later, he is turned in to the proper authorities in NYC.

I may have been off work for a while, but my return tonight has gotten at least one bad guy put behind bars. Now, on to the next one…

Chapter Nine
Blaze

Everything comes to a head on an unusually cold day in December. I have a *hellish* day at work. I lose two straight cases when they go to court, meaning all my work to prepare for them was for nothing. Then, I get absolutely reamed out by the Captain, for a whole variety of things, including both the court losses and giving up on the prostitution ring. My favorite lunch place gets my order wrong, and then when I go to leave for the day, my tire is flat. By the time I finally get home, feeling exhausted and fighting a burgeoning headache, all I want is Ari. It's not even that I want to have sex, either. I want to see Ari's smile up close, chocolate dimples sinking, beautiful, thick lips spreading into a glorious sight. I want to lay with my head in Ari's lap and listen to her tell me that tomorrow will be a better day. I want all of her. I take a single second to marvel at how well and truly fucked I am. Then, I pick up the phone, find her name, and hit dial. Ari answers after only a single ring.

"Hello?" her sweet voice purrs on the line.

Even the sound of her voice is comforting. It washes over me, bathing me in warmth. I close my eyes and take several breaths, letting myself finally relax.

"Blaze? Are you there?" Ari asks.

"Yes." I glance over at the time. It's early in the evening when she is usually working, so it doesn't seem like an appropriate time to ask her to meet me. Still, I swallow my pride and say, "I need to see you." It comes out in a rush. "I'm sure you're busy, but I need to see you."

I start to tell her I will pay her for any time lost with her clients, but she answers, "I'll be there soon. I just need to wrap up at work."

That makes my stomach lurch—the constant reminder of Ari's *work*. If Ari is leaving a client early for me though, then I need to be happy about that. That's the best I'm going to get with a woman in her profession. I knew what I signed up for before I fell for her. But still, it doesn't stop the pangs of jealousy from biting at my manhood.

Less than thirty minutes later, there's a knock on the door. Ari is on the other side, hands tucked into the dense shell of her jacket.

"Fuck, Ari," I breathe out, blinking at the sight. There's snow dusting Ari's brown curls. She looks ethereal, otherworldly, with her honey brown skin contrasted against her glowing hazel eyes. "I can't believe you came this fast."

"Why wouldn't I?" she asks. "You said you needed to see me."

I close the short distance between us, curling both hands around the back of Ari's neck and letting both thumbs brush Ari's jaw. Then, I kiss her until I can barely breathe anymore, feeling all of the tension melt out of my body.

This isn't about shielding Ari from the law anymore. I'll do horrible things for her—would break even more laws for her, besides the one she's already made her peace with. It would scare me a little if I didn't see the same magnitude of feelings reflected in Ari's eyes when she steps away, catching her breath.

"I missed you," I tell her.

Ari reaches up, laying a hand over one of mine resting on my neck. "My name is Yandy," she says quietly. "Yandy Martin."

"Yandy?" I repeat, liking the way it rolls off my tongue.

"Is Ari a working name or something?" I ask her. I had figured long ago she would use a different name for her clients, and I feel honored she revealed to me the name of the real person beyond her profession.

"Yes. It's my middle name, and I use it for work," she admits.

I kiss Yandy again, heartfelt, fully able to appreciate the magnitude of the trust it shows for her to be so honest with me. I keep kissing Yandy, too, until I feel the sharp sting of a punch to my arm.

"Ow!" I complain, rubbing at the spot. "What was that for?"

"Since I'm being honest, I want you to be honest too. What's your name?" Yandy demands. "Blaze is a hot name, but what's your real one?"

I grin. Right, I'd kind of forgotten Yandy didn't already know this. She probably thinks I gave her a fake name, too.

"It actually is Blaze," I say. "Blaze Wells. You've been calling me the right name all along."

Yandy snorts a bark of laughter, even though her eyebrows knit with something strange.

"You should pick a better pseud next time, Blaze."

"There won't be a next time," I tell her sincerely.

She takes the hidden message from what I'm saying. "I hope not. I don't want there to be anyone other than you either," she mutters.

"Stop working then. Stay with me," I whisper near her ear as I bite down on her earlobe. "I will take care of you, now and forever. All that I have, I will share with you." None of what I'm saying is planned, so I know it's coming from a sincere place. I want this woman here with me, and I want her forever.

"Blaze, what I do is more complicated than you think."

"If someone is making you go out there, tell me his name. I will get rid of him by tomorrow. Trust me, I have my ways," I tell her, my blood boiling over at the thought of someone forcing her to sell her body.

"I will tell you everything, soon," she says and leans into me, kissing my lips.

"Tell me now," I breathe out, then breathe in her intoxicating scent. I regularly dream of becoming one with her, and this moment is no different as my cock springs to life over the aroma of her invigorating scent.

"In due time, Blaze."

I decide not to press her, knowing she reveals everything on her own time anyway.

"I want you naked, Yandy," I say, loving the way her real name sounds rolling off my tongue. "I want you naked and in my bed."

"Not as much as I want you naked and in the bed," she says and begins to strip out of her clothes.

I help her out of her jacket, then step back to watch her peel off a purple sweater dress. I want to help her with her clothes too, but that would ruin the beauty of her doing it nice and slow right in front of my eyes. I feel like the luckiest man alive when she stands before me wearing only her purple panties.

"Blaze, now that I'm naked, what are you going to do with me?" she asks in a sultry voice. A clear sign that she aches for me to be buried deep inside of her as much as I ache to be inside of her. That detail sends a healthy flow of blood to my manhood, and he's fully ready.

"Oh, I can think of some things to do to you," I say.

"Is that so?" she asks, turning around to bend and take off her panties seductively. Her butt cheeks spread beautifully. Then, she backs her ass up to press against my cock.

I feel like a caveman trying to relieve myself of my pants and boxers as quickly as humanly possible.

She looks back at me and giggles, but before she can get a good laugh in my hardness is resting against her slick entrance. I grip her hips and thrust into her, reuniting us in our most perfect union by sheathing my manhood with her tight, gushy center. This is our first time uniting without a barrier, and it feels like heaven.

She moans out my name, the sound alone making me give her my all. I growl against her ear as I lean into her and write my name all over her walls. She will remember no man other than me if it's the last thing I do while here on Earth.

"Blaze, I love...this...so much," she murmurs, barely able to speak the words clearly.

I plunge into her heat over and over again, biting down on my bottom lip as I try not to explode from the feel of taking her without a barrier. Yandy is soft inside, and her juices coat my manhood and leak down her legs and mine.

When Yandy starts to tremble, gripping my manhood with every tremor, I can no longer hold it together. I ram into her core, filling her up with every ounce of cum I have to offer with each blow.

"Stay with me," I mutter between each stroke. I may be going mad, but I want her with me as insanity takes me to a place I've never been before meeting Yandy. No future moments should pass where we are not together. I don't want her out on the streets. She should be here with me.

A loud moan escapes her sensual throat. "Yes!" Her body shudders, and she cries out as each wave of orgasm devours her alive.

I pull out of her and stand up straight, pulling her up with me. I stammer to the couch and sit down, bringing her down onto my lap, where I devour her lips, drinking from her mouth until I am full.

"Yandy, were you answering my question or were those cries of pleasure."

"A little bit of both," she whispers, breathlessly. "I have my own place, so maybe we should start dating before we do the move in thing."

"Oh, baby. We are so far beyond dating, and I know all I need to know about you. I want you here," I tell her, meaning it from the pits of my soul. I am done doing the visit thing; we belong together.

She kisses my lips to quiet me. I forget my train of thought momentarily as a kiss like the one she's delivering to my lips is designed to do. It's a warm embrace of two sets of heated souls meant to change worldviews and convert a man from bachelorhood to being hooked to the ball and chain. I'll come back to the conversation of making her stay with me forever. For the moment, I'm enchanted by the feel of her sinking into my soul and me into hers.

Chapter Ten
Yandy

Blaze convinces me to stay the night. Well, it doesn't take much convincing after he brands my body twice more in an attempt to get me to agree to live with him. Finally, after I'm so limp that I feel like a limp noodle, he allows me to rest.

Late into the night, I'm woken up by two phones going off in unison. Both are playing the standard Apple ringtone, but slightly off from each other, making for a jarring contrast. Blaze's hands slide on my warm, naked skin when he leans across the bed to fetch his work iPhone.

"Hello, this is Blaze," he answers groggily.

Next to him, my sleepy voice is raspy when I answer my phone and ask, "What can I do for you?"

"Agent Martin," the person on the other line says curtly. "There's a situation I want to make sure you are aware of, in case you get called for back-up."

"What's going on?" I ask, jarring more awake with each passing second.

My superior starts running down the details to me, and I'm in shock of what's going on with the trafficking ring I've been trying to bring down. Apparently, they just got a new boost to their circle, and it's a more disgusting set of circumstances than I could've ever imagined. Stomach churning, my limbs are thrumming with adrenaline, making me think it's going to be a long time before I get back to a bed to sleep. There has been an influx of young Mexican girls who were separated at the border from their parents that were here for asylum. The US government lost track of the girls, and now the young, most vulnerable group of teenagers are being pimped in the streets of New York City. I'm entirely enraged by the time I hang up the phone. When Blaze ends his call, he equally looks like a bundle of nerves.

"Yandy," Blaze says urgently. His anxious tone overwhelms how I'm already feeling. "I don't want to tell you to stop seeing clients, but you can't go back out there. The New York Police are beginning a massive raid this week. They're going to be arresting hundreds of people, and one of them could be you if you go back out there, especially since I found you so easily," he says.

I stare at him confused over what seems like an awkward statement. My mouth is half open in shock and awe. "What do you mean by saying you found me easily? What are you saying, Blaze?"

"I couldn't stand it if something happens to you," Blaze continues, clenching his chest. "I don't want to be put in a position of putting my job on the line to keep you out of jail, but I know I'll do it if it comes down to it, so let's just not put ourselves in that position, okay?"

"What the hell?" I say, sitting up straighter.

"I'm sorry," Blaze insists. "I haven't been entirely honest with you. I work for the New York PD. I'm a cop, and that was someone in my department warning me about the future busts about to happen to prostitutes all over the city, and especially in the area near the park where you work. They're not looking for you, but there have been a lot of girls coming in from Mexico, and we have to get to the bottom of it."

"What the hell?" I repeat, sitting up and looking at him as if he has two heads. How did I miss the detail that he's a cop? At this moment, I know I fell for him the second I saw him because there is no way in hell this should be coming to me as a surprise right now. Researching people and their motives is what I do. "Break this down to me like I'm a two-year-old, what are you saying exactly?" I ask, not wanting to believe I've been sleeping with a cop. Not that it's a bad thing; it is actually great news, but how could I have been tricked? I should know better than this.

My mind is stunned by the fact that he's not a John, and we didn't start out as a trick and a prostitute with me being just some random piece of cheap ass he was willing to pay for. He goes out there to clean the streets just as I do. He's a good man through and through, and not someone looking to exploit a prostitute. Everything about this revelation is giving me new life.

"I should never have started this thing to begin with, but I couldn't help myself. I was drawn to you, and I didn't want to let you go, Yandy. I'm so sorry I've been lying to you, but I just couldn't figure out how to clean things up once it got started," Blaze continues, willing me to believe him by the sincerity in his eyes. "I didn't want to lose you."

"No, you don't understand," I say, waving for him to stop talking. "You just stole my line. I just got off the phone with my boss, and I was going to tell *you* to be careful tonight."

Blaze drops his phone. "I don't understand what you're saying. Speak to me like I'm a two-year-old," he uses my line.

"I was about to warn you that we're going to be arresting any Blazes we find this week, men out soliciting for sex. I was worried about you getting arrested by my team."

"You're a cop?" he asks, disbelievingly.

"*You're* a cop," I shoot back, smiling, relief substantially more pronounced than the shock.

"Wow, this is a lot to take in. But the first thing I want to say is I have no intention of going out there to pick up anyone else. I have all the woman I need right here." I smile as Blaze pauses to think. "Were you going to let me pay you for sex and never say anything about being a cop? Shitty police work, Ari," he retorts.

"You were going to pay me for sex and not arrest me!" I counter. "You suck at your job, too!" I start giggling, and before long, we are both tickled to death over finding out we're both undercover.

"Maybe it's not that we suck, it's just that we were meant to suck on each other," he says, pulling me closer to him and kissing my neck, while suckling at my skin. "I'm glad this is out in the open. Now, we can start something serious without any inhibitions," he adds.

I'm still naked in his bed, sheets pooling around my waist. I gaze into his eyes; then, my eyes roam over his body. There's a rash of red at the base of his neck from where I left my mark earlier in the night. He's strong and gorgeous, and I don't have to feel guilty for wanting to be with him any longer. This is a good thing.

"Yes, we can," I surrender to the idea of being with him freely. "And, I would love that."

"So, you don't have other clients?" he asks again as if that bit of knowledge gives him life. "Just me?"

"No! I don't have clients, at all. You're not even a client, you're my boo," I say and chuckle loudly.

He chuckles with me. "I'll take that. I'll take *all* of that," he says, pulling me back into his arms and holding me there for what seems like the longest time.

"You don't go picking up hookers on the reg?" I ask to clear the air. I guess that's something I'm hung up on too.

"Fuck no!" he says, leaning back on the bed. "I fuckin' hated that assignment when I got it. It took me so long to figure out what to wear, thus Terry's suit, and then I didn't know what to say, how to hold my hands...it was a disaster."

"God, me too," I say and start laughing, a choked off, wheezing sound that's pretty contagious.

Blaze starts chuckling along with me.

"I hate going undercover doing this, but the FBI wanted me to go deep cover, so I've been doing this for a few months. We've been trying to figure out the flow of girls caught up in this sex trafficking ring," I admit.

"You're amazing!" he says while tugging at my bottom lip.

"You're pretty amazing too," I tell him. "But the most amazing part is that now we can get out there and fight this problem together."

"Most definitely," he says, his finger now running circles over my shoulders. "These assholes don't have a chance now."

"No chance," I agree.

"You know we're going to have to come up with a very different story for how we started dating," he says, still running circles over my skin which heats up in every place he touches. "My mom can never hear this one," he adds before his lips come crashing down on mine warming me to the core.

"Neither can mine," I say, giggling, imagining the day Blaze would meet my parents and impress them with his charm just as he amazes me with the way he expresses his love for me. "Do you think your mother will like me because I can tell you now my parents are going to love everything about you?" I ask.

"Baby, my mother has said so many prayers that I will meet a girl as brilliant, compassionate and lovely as you. If she doesn't fall head over heels in love with you, then I don't know what to say. What's not to love about you?" Blaze says as he climbs on top of me, covering my body with his.

While I can think of some obvious barriers to his mother accepting me, I clear my mind as we make the sweetest love with our full truth on the line. We give ourselves to each other wholeheartedly for the first time.

And, as the future holds, Blaze is right. When I meet his mother, she makes me feel right at home and a part of the family. My mother falls head over heels in love with him, and he passes my father's test for a man capable of taking care of his daughter. Our love life is on the right path. We have everything we desire, finally.

Epilogue
Blaze

Six Months Later

When I step out of my car and head to the alley, I see her before I get there. The light mist in the air is reminiscent of the first day we met and makes what I'm about to do even more meaningful. I make my way across the street towards the alley, anxious to be close to her. As soon as she sees me, she presses her back against the old stone wall and props one foot on an old stump for support. She knows I love it when she sees me coming and stands in that nasty way that drives me wild.

"Are you looking for a good time?" she starts our cat and mouse game.

"No," I say, startling her. "Not tonight. I need more than that from you tonight."

This is different from the role-playing routine we have done dozens of times. I'm supposed to proposition her with the idea of riding my cock cowboy style behind one of these buildings. She's supposed to tell me I have to cook her dinner. Then, we're supposed to run off deeper into the alley and fuck like rabbits with the possibility of getting caught by the old lady, which excites us both to no end.

"What…what do you want to do then?" she plays along until I drop down on one knee. That's when her eyes start glowing brightly.

"I have the best proposition for you yet," I say.

"Oh really? What's that?" she counters with a glimmer of lust in her eyes. I can see the wheels turning in her mind as she contemplates what kind of excursion I'm about to take her on.

"I want you to be mine, officially. Will you be my wife, Yandy Ari Martin? Will you marry me?"

"Blaze, are you serious?" she whispers.

"Yes," I say and produce a ring from my back pocket. "I'm very serious."

"Oh, my…Yes. I will marry you. Yes! Yes! I will."

I begin to slide the ring onto her finger.

"Hurry up and put it on so I can kiss you already," she demands.

I stand up and take her into my arms, and we melt together, my lips crashing down onto hers. "Thank you, for making me the happiest man alive."

"Thank goodness," the old lady says from a window behind us. "It's about time somebody married that girl. Poor thing's been out here for months trying to catch somebody's attention. Now, will you take her to your house so she can stop loitering in front of my building? Make an honest woman out of her for everybody's sake in this building."

"Mind your business!" I say, angrily. For some reason, I take the old lady's words to heart, even though she doesn't know what she's talking about.

"No, what she's saying is true, Blaze. Thank goodness, you're making an honest woman out of me. With this ring, you can have me all night every night. You can take me to your apartment and do all kinds of things to me, along with taking me up against the alley wall," Yandy says in a tease.

"Oh, goodness, he's going to give you a place to stay too," the lady says jokingly. "You better get going now, girl."

"Hey, what are you two doing?" Sloane asks in a grunting whisper as he walks up. "Are you trying to run all the action off from this block, or what? This isn't love connection. She's working," he adds with an attitude as he glares at me with contempt.

"So, I've been meaning to talk to you for a while now. The first thing we need to clear up is, when you see me talking to my woman, there is no reason for you to step forward and say a damn thing. I can and will protect my woman from any issues that may arise. Secondly, I know she's working, but she's a grown woman and can speak to me when she wants me to leave her alone," I bark at Sloane.

I don't give a damn if he's upset about seeing me out there with Yandy. He knows we're a couple, and I don't like the way he's always butting in with an opinion. This conversation is long overdue. He's too protective of my woman, and I'm the only man she needs to protect her.

Ever since I started dating Yandy officially, I've been watching her back out here. In coordination with the FBI, we've taken hundreds, if not thousands, of men off the streets in the past six months. My main concern each day is not only bringing criminals to justice and rescuing young girls who may be forced to be out here, but also to make sure no one harms a hair on my woman's head. That is my job now, and it's time Sloane gets it through his thick skull.

"I don't know what she sees in a punk like you anyway. Fucking NYPD?" Sloane says on a laugh.

I can feel the veins in my head swell until they're about to pop out. This guy doesn't know he's close to catching an ass whipping like it's the flu.

"Sloane, you are out of line!" Yandy yells and then pushes her partner in the chest. "What the hell is your problem?"

"Why are you coming after me? Talk to the cop about how he's out of line for being out here. For fucks sake, he should know as well as we do that you don't come on an undercover prostitute's corner proposing marriage. That shit is whack as

115

hell," Sloane yells back at Yandy while looking incredulous.

"Back off, Sloane!" she urges.

"No, I won't back off! I've been here for you for years, and he strolls in, and now you're in love?" He stands close in her face as he speaks. The way he is looking at her makes me lose what's left of my mind.

I step to him and push him out of her face; then, I land a good shiner onto his right eye. "Don't you ever stand flat-footed in front of my woman and yell at her. Do you fucking understand me, *boy*?" I say, punching him again.

He strikes back, somehow maneuvering to his feet. "She's more my woman than she is yours. I care about her more than you do."

"Oh my god. That went downhill fast, but this is juicy stuff. Who will the prostitute choose, the handsome lover boy or the man who's always stalking her?" the old lady yells from her window.

"Shut up!" we all yell to her at once.

She quickly closes her window after talking about how she's about to call the cops.

"Sloane, I am not yours, and you know that already. Blaze just proposed to me, and you, of all

116

people, should be happy for me," Yandy tells her partner.

"How can I be happy seeing you with him? When I've wanted you since the moment I laid eyes on you? The only reason I didn't say anything was that you're my partner, and I try to be professional, but seeing you out here frolicking around with him, and now accepting his proposal, lets me know it's time I let you know how I feel. I love you, Yandy," Sloane pours his heart out.

"It doesn't matter how you feel," I say, stepping in front of Yandy to protect her. "She is mine!" I yell, not caring who hears my pronouncement of her being mine.

Yandy moves around me and touches my chest. Her touch soothes me a bit, so I let out a deep sigh. "Hold up, Blaze. I can handle Sloane," she assures me with a look in her eyes letting me know I can relax a little and let her handle it. Still, I'm on edge. "As soon as I get into the station in the morning, I'm asking to be taken off this assignment and to be assigned to a new partner. There is no way we can work together any longer," she tells him curtly.

"Oh yeah?" Sloane asks. "If you're going to go in there and tell them about me, make sure you tell them everything you've been doing the past eight months."

I move toward Sloane again, and Yandy pulls me back. I'm ready to spaz over what was supposed to be a freakishly beautiful moment turning into a war with her partner. But, I've always had a feeling his supposed protectiveness of his partner was something much more profound. Take him seeing her home every night, for example. Even though the man knows I'm there for her, he still stalks around her house at unwanted times of the night. Now, the cat is out of the bag, his feelings are exposed for all to see.

"Tell them what you want, Sloane. I'm asking for a new partner tomorrow, *and* I'm marrying Blaze."

***

Yandy

In all the time I have known Sloane, I've known him to be a domineering man, always having to be in control of every situation he encounters. Yet, I never knew he wanted to be with

118

me intimately. To hear him out here professing his feelings, after Blaze proposed to me, is mindboggling.

I talk Blaze into taking me back to his place, but it's hard to get him to drop it with Sloane. He looks like he wants to kill him as we walk away. We slide into Blaze's blue SUV and ride to his apartment in silence.

"Has he ever touched you?" is the first question out of Blaze's mouth as soon as his front door closes with him pinning me against it.

"No, never," I say. "But you already know that."

"It just makes me want to smash something, knowing he came out there intending to start something with me. You know we've never clicked," Blaze admits. "I've always been courteous to him, but I never really clicked with him. It was like something was holding him back from being cordial, so I dropped it. I'm not here for him anyway."

"You should have told me you had those feelings about him. Maybe I would have seen it sooner," I surmise, though I know this is no one's fault but Sloane's. What he did was uncalled for.

"I don't like to insinuate things I'm not sure of. It was just a nagging feeling I had," Blaze admits.

"You know what? Enough about him. You proposed to me," I said smiling.

"Yes, and now that that's been tainted, I'm going to have to figure out another way to surprise you and do it all over again. I want it to be perfect. You know, middle of a dark alley type of perfect for us."

I chuckle. "Oh Blaze, it was wonderful. No one can take that away from us."

"I wanted to take you somewhere and celebrate in public. You know how we do," he insinuates, causing me to grin widely.

I look over at his balcony window. "I see the perfect place for us to celebrate right here, right now."

He smiles at me wickedly.

I run over to the window with him following close behind me. Before I reach it, he spins me around and starts kissing me.

"I love your mind, pretty woman," he says, his hands reaching down to cup my ass.

Blaze helps me out of my clothes, and I help him out of his. I marvel over the sight in front of me; my man is fine. Scratch that, my future husband is sexy as hell. I feel like I've won a prize that grants me the ability to see all of this beautiful nakedness every day for the rest of my life. I'm such a lucky girl.

"Blaze, now that we have our clothes off, what's next?" I ask in a teasing way.

His eyes glaze over, a clear sign that he aches to be buried deep inside of me. "You're making me want you even more than I did before. How is this even possible?" he asks.

"I don't know." I sashay over to the window and bend over in front of it, leaving my ass tooted up for Blaze to consider whether he wants to talk about his desires or indulge in them. I look back at him and wiggle my finger at him in a come hither motion.

"Oh my god, woman!" he growls, and within seconds, he's all over me, his hardness resting against my slick entrance.

"You're going to get me pregnant if you keep sexing me raw," I tell him, to which his reply is to grip my hips and thrust so deep inside of me that I gasp for air. Reuniting with Blaze is the next best thing close to a slice of heaven.

"I want you pregnant. I want you to have all of my babies," he growls out as he thrusts inside of me.

All? I think, but I can barely tell the difference between my eyelids and the street down beneath us as he moves in and out of me.

"Blaze. Oh, baby," I moan out his name as he claims me with each stroke. It is no doubt in my mind that I belong to him and he belongs to me. "I love you so much! Oh, I love you, Big Blaze!"

"I love you more," he mutters, bending over to drop the words close to my ear. He plunges into my heat over and over again, biting down on my shoulders as I try not to explode from the feel of him filling me completely.

"Ask me again," I murmur.

"What, baby? Oh, baby, you feel so good," he murmurs.

"Ask me again," I say, gripping his cock within my walls tightly.

"Yandy, baby. Yandy—Ari," he says, sounding as if he's about to succumb to our passionate lovemaking. "You're driving me mad!"

"Ask me!" I grip his manhood tighter.

"Will you marry me? Baby, please will you marry me?" he says as he grunts his pleasures loudly.

After hearing his proposal, I can feel my juices flowing out of me and running down my legs. I'm seconds away from squirting all over his floor.

"Yes! Yes, I will marry you," I say, trembling and gripping onto his manhood with every tremor. I give him myself freely, and all of me, saving nothing for myself. He rams into my heated core, taking all that I have and depositing his all, along with our future baby inside of me.

"Say you'll stay with me, forever," he mutters as he spins me around into his arms.

"Forever," I murmur.

"I mean it, Yandy. I want no moments to pass where we are not together. I want you with me, forever."

"I'm not going anywhere," I say and hold him close to me. "I'm yours."

He kisses my lips; a kiss meant to hold me right there, rendering me unable to move from that very spot for as long as he wants me there.

I don't want to think or feel anything else for as long as I live. No one and nothing can tear us apart, and our purpose to make the world a better place will only bring us closer together. Right now, all I want is to be right here with Blaze to experience moments such as this.

THE END

UPDATE ON THE DANGEROUS BONDS SERIES:

Safe Place 1 & 2 will be combined into one book that will release on my birthday May 21st!

Read Dangerous Bonds Now

Made in the USA
Las Vegas, NV
09 October 2021